Smugglers' Snugglers Snowy Play

by Mary Kay Sloan

Special thanks to Barbara Thomke, who made this book possible.

This book is dedicated with love to my Smugglers' Snugglers: Chris, Kelsey, Amanda, and Lauren.

In memory of Vincent Sloan, whose favorite place was Smugglers' Notch Resort.

To order additional copies of this book, contact:
Xlibris Corporation
1-888-795-4274
www.Xlibris.com
Orders@Xlibris.com

It's snowy at Smugglers'! What a great day!
All kinds of Snugglers come here to play.
There's so much to do in the powdery snow.
Follow the footprints. Dress snuggly and go!

"Follow me," says bear to his furry new friend.

He scampers uphill and around the next bend.

"My very first snow!" calls the cub. See him run!

"Come catch me!" he calls. "I love snow—this is fun!"

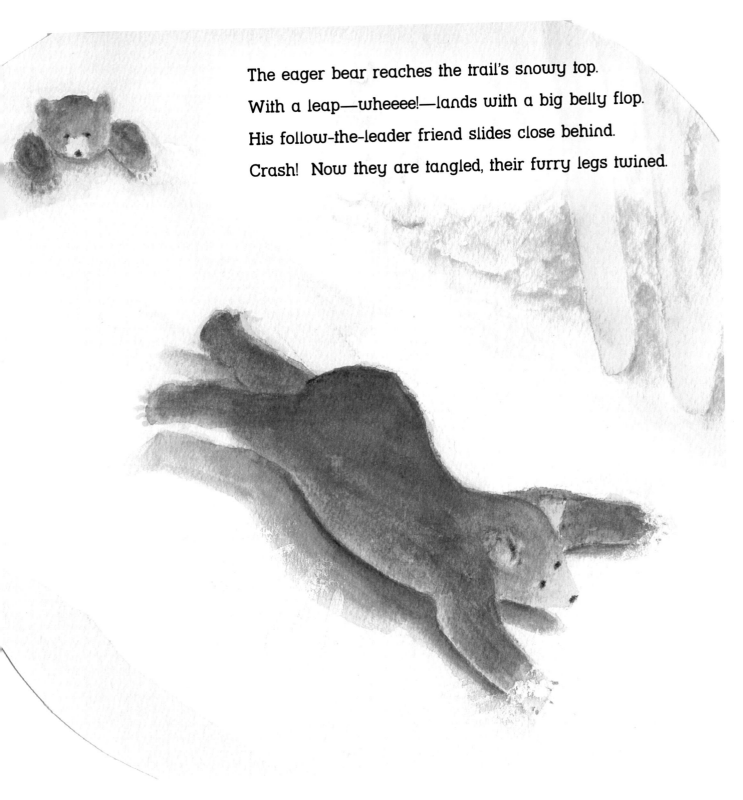

The eager bear reaches the trail's snowy top.

With a leap—wheeee!—lands with a big belly flop.

His follow-the-leader friend slides close behind.

Crash! Now they are tangled, their furry legs twined.

The burly bears tumble and roll head to toe,
Down Meadowlark Trail. "Look out below!"
Over and over they roll as they fall.
Faster and faster—a furry snowball!

At the end of the trail, they slide to a stop.

They're too tired to climb way back up to the top.

Shaking flakes from their fur, wiping snow from their eyes,

They reach up their paws for big bear high fives.

MEADOWLARK
TRAIL

They lumber away to a cave to the west,
Snuggling together for a long winter's rest.

"Follow me, follow me," says the white snowshoe hare.

"We have really big feet—but we really don't care!"

If you've ever worn snowshoes, then you would know,

That they never, no never, get stuck in the snow!

The snowshoe hares' feet are made perfect for play;
Slip-sliding on Sterling Pond, every which way.
Their long ears flap out as they hold their paws tight,
Spinning in circles, one left and one right.

Faster and faster, spinning up and around,

Their enormous feet actually lift off the ground.

Twirling, the dancing continues until

A bump in the ice—whoa!—a snowshoe hare spill!

Zipping on ice, they slide into the snow,

Covered with snowflakes from ear-tops to toe.

On big snowshoe feet, they're like snowy ghost trees.

"Brrr … we're so cold! Can we head for home, please?"

They hop hop-a-long to their warm cozy house,
Uphill, past the lift skiers call Mogul Mouse.

"Follow me," says the deer. "Please come play "hide-and-seek."

"Follow me to Madonna and Sterling's high peak."

Where the snowghost trees sh-sh-shiver and shake,

Chasing down Thomke's Trail and leaping Black Snake.

Their white tails bob, they make hardly a sound,

Their hoofed feet barely touch the ground.

When on the ski trail giant moguls appear,

Then they're up and away like Santa's reindeer.

"Oh no! Now how are we going to stop?"
They shimmie and slide, and then kerplop!
Their long slender legs splay out east and west.
On pillows of snow, heads go down for a rest.

As they rise, one is wearing a purple ski hat!

Dotted with snow, a child's lost cap.

"Look!" The deer say when they're ready to go,

"Behind we left angels imprinted in snow."

They leap through the meadows past Red Fox Glades,
To snuggle together as last daylight fades.

"Woo-hoo! Fresh snow! Which trail should we ski?"
Calls the young Snuggler, "Come, come, follow me!"
Eager to ski and board every tall peak.
So much to do—but in only one week?

Starting with ski camp and then "cookie race,"

Off through the glades, playing "catch me" and "chase."

At Superpipe learning the funky corkscrew,

To jam and swing with the boarding crew.

When the lifts close, there's still more to do:
Snugglers skate or tube or cross-country ski, too.
Snowshoe through the woods by the silver moonlight,
And spot tracks of furry friends, hiding from sight.

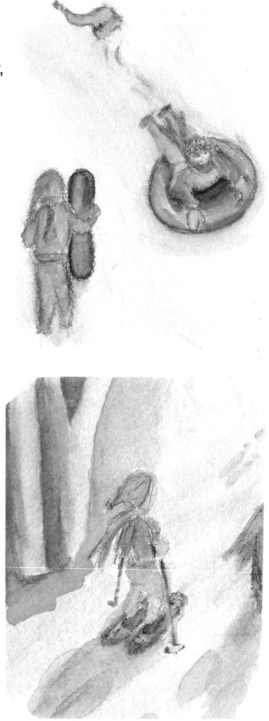

Snugglers snuggle around the bonfire aglow,

With tales of our fun day and mmmm... hot cocoa!

For fireworks and torchlight parade, let's cheer!

Marking the calendar for the same trip next year.

With ONE hat still on, Snugglers turn out the light.
All SMUGGLERS' SNUGGLERS will sleep soundly tonight.

OUR FAVORITE SMUGGLERS' NOTCH MEMORIES

_____

_____

_____

_____

_____

_____

_____

_____

_____

_____

_____

_____

_____

_____

_____

_____

_____

_____

_____

_____

_____